For Endaf.
With special thanks to Helen Mortimer, Sarah Darby,
and Jason Taylor for their creative support.

Sisters Nicola and Charlotte

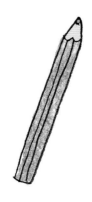

Text and illustrations copyright © 2012 by Charlotte Middleton
Nibbles' Garden: Another Green Tale was originally published in England in 2012 as **Christopher's Caterpillars**.
This edition is published by arrangement with Oxford University Press.
First Marshall Cavendish edition, 2012

Marshall Cavendish Corporation
99 White Plains Road
Tarrytown, NY 10591
www.marshallcavendish.us/kids

Library of Congress Cataloging-in-Publication Data
Middleton, Charlotte.
Nibbles' garden : another green tale / by Charlotte Middleton. – 1st Marshall Cavendish ed.
p. cm.
Summary: When Nibbles the guinea pig and his friend Posie find caterpillars munching on
their prize-winning dandelion plants, they decide to make the caterpillars their pets.
ISBN 978-0-7614-6134-0 (hardcover)
[1. Caterpillars–Fiction. 2. Butterflies–Fiction. 3. Metamorphosis–Fiction. 4. Guinea pigs–Fiction.] I. Title.
PZ7.M5845Nj 2012
[E]–dc23
2011016341

The illustrations are rendered in mixed media.
Book design by Virginia Pope
Editor: Robin Benjamin

Printed in China (P)
10 9 8 7 6 5 4 3 2 1

 **Marshall Cavendish** Children

Nibbles' Garden

Another Green Tale

Written and illustrated by
Charlotte Middleton

Marshall Cavendish Children

If there was one thing Nibbles **loved** almost as much as playing soccer, it was gardening.

Nibbles' dandelions were the tastiest in the whole of Dandeville. They had even won prizes.

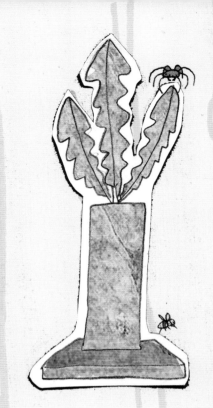

But growing prize-winning plants . . .

was too much work for one guinea pig.

So Nibbles was very happy
when he met his new neighbor, Posie.

Nibbles and Posie worked
in the garden together.

They also played soccer and went on picnics.
Soon they became best friends.

One day, Nibbles heard a strange
sound coming from his dandelions.

munch

crunch

crunch

munch

crunch

crunch

SIX VERY HAIRY CATERPILLARS
were eating his prize plants!

as pets! Nibbles and Posie wrote
a list of all the things they might need
to look after their caterpillars.

little woolly socks

glasses of milk and
jelly beans

Ping-Pong balls
(for playing soccer)

small hairbrushes

And they took it to Mr. Rosetti in the café. He knew everything about everything.

Mr. Rosetti looked at the list and made a few suggestions.

- ✗ little woolly socks
- ✓ clean jars
- ✗ glasses of milk and jelly beans
- ✓ juicy leaves for munching
- ✗ Ping-Pong balls (for playing soccer)
- ✓ twigs for climbing
- ✗ small hairbrushes
- ✓ lids with holes for plenty of fresh air

He even had some clean jars to give
to Nibbles and Posie. He told them
how to look after their new pets
so they'd know exactly what to do.

Nibbles and Posie loved their new pets.

They were the happiest caterpillars in Dandeville.

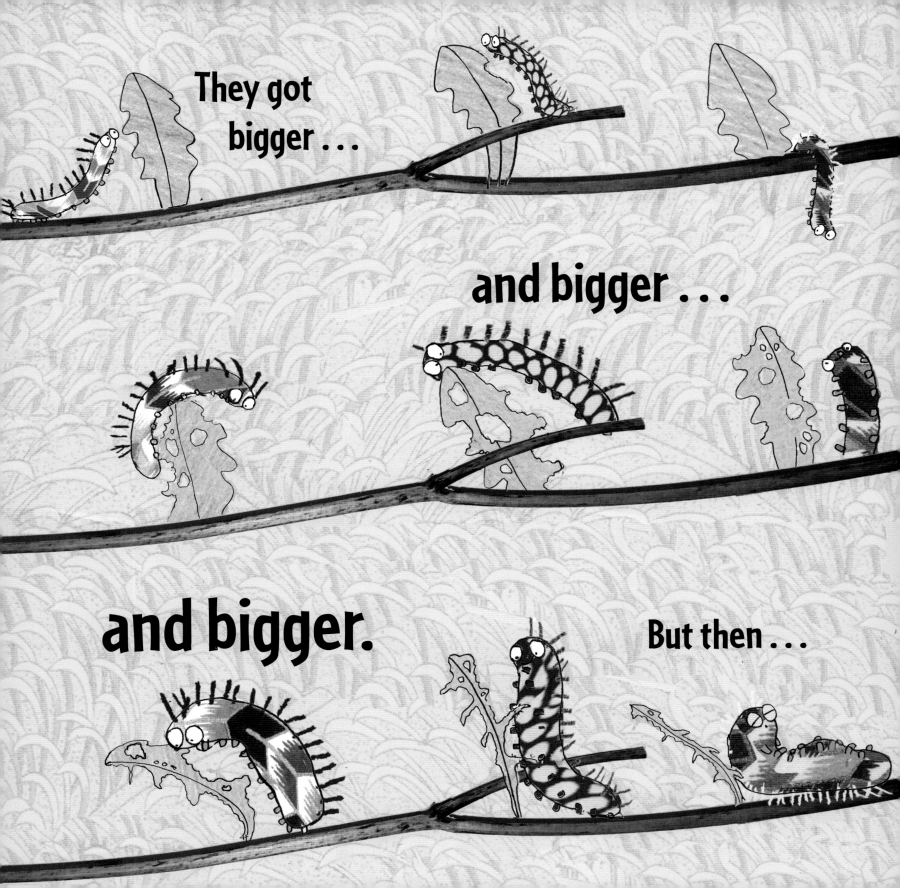

they were gone!

Not a single wriggling caterpillar to be seen.
Not a single munching sound to be heard.

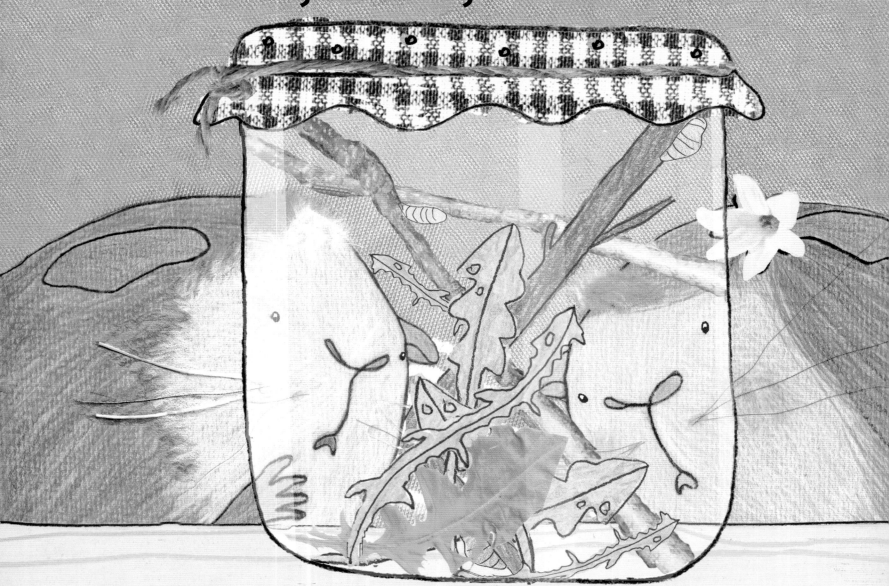

It was **quite a mystery**.

Nibbles and Posie were determined
to solve the mystery of their missing pets.
They made some posters...

and put them up
all over Dandeville.

DANDEVILLE BAKERY

OPEN

LOST!
six caterpillars

HAVE YOU SEEN THEM?

Posie and Nibbles were worried. Nobody had seen their caterpillars.

Then an e-mail from Mr. Rosetti popped up in Nibbles' inbox.

From: Mr. ROSETTI
To: NIBBLES
Subject: Lost Caterpillars!

Please bring your jars to the café.

six beautiful butterflies.

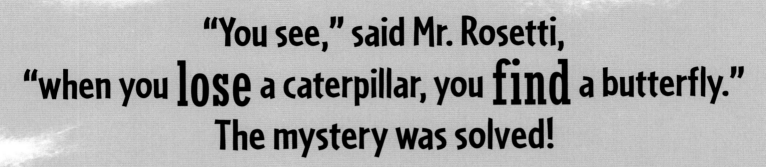

"You see," said Mr. Rosetti,
"when you **lose** a caterpillar, you **find** a butterfly."
The mystery was solved!

Nibbles and Posie
made some new
posters . . .

so that the guinea pigs of
Dandeville would know
what had happened
to the caterpillars.

The posters that
Nibbles and Posie made were so nice . . .

FOUN

they were hung in the Dandeville Art Gallery
for everyone to see.

LOST!
six caterpillars

HAVE YOU

FOUND!